High-Frequency
READERS™

We Can Go!

Written by Ellen Geist

Illustrated by Ken Bowser

Scholastic Inc.
New York   Toronto   London   Auckland   Sydney
Mexico City   New Delhi   Hong Kong

ISBN 0-439-13988-0

11 10 9 8

5/0
62

Printed in China

First Scholastic clubs printing, November 1999

We can go to the library.

I can go to the mountains.

I can go to the desert.

I can go to the North Pole.

I can go to the ocean.

I can go to the jungle.

We can go to the moon!